Come and play with us!

Illustrated by Annie Kubler and Caroline Formby

Published by Child's Play (International) Ltd
Swindon Auburn ME Sydney

ISBN 0-85953-793-5 Printed in China
This impression 2005 Library of Congress Number 96-47796
A catalogue reference for this book is available from the British Library

ALBANIA

It's cold in the mountains where these children live.
They are playing in the school sports ground.

**I'm Agim. I'm making kites.
Hey, Roland, your kite is ready
Who else would like a kite?**

Hello.
I'm Nathan.

JAMAICA

It is warm and sunny in the Caribbean.
After school the children head for the beach.

**I'm Nathan. My sister Evelyn and I are reading.
Look, Marjorie and Vera have surf boards.
Come on, Evelyn, you can finish your book later.
It's much more fun in the water.
Isn't it?**

I'm Anna. I can do magic.
How many dolls can you see, Rudi? One?
Wrong! Shut your eyes.
Open! Look, there are seven!
Where did they come from?

RUSSIA Children play a lot indoors.
Grandparents often look after them.

I'm Tommy. I love basketball.
Look out, Grace!
Someone's behind you!
Pass it to me!
I won't miss!

USA
Even in the most crowded city,
you will find kids playing basketball.

SOUTH AFRICA

These children live in a township outside Cape Town.
They don't have money to spend on toys,
so they make their own.

I'm Zolani. I made this car,
and Zinzi's and Sipho's toys, too.
We're going to race them.
Bring me some wire
and I'll show you how to make one.
Then you can race, too. I bet mine wins!

88 ... 89 ... 90. I am Lajana. Look how high I can jump.
Hey, Menna, let's swap your hoop for my rope.
My friend from Australia taught me to hula-hoop.
Do you want me to show you how?

NEPAL

This is one of the highest parts of the world.
Imagine playing with mountains all around!

SOUTH SUDAN
There's plenty of space to run around,
but sometimes it's just too hot.

I'm Abe. That's me kicking the ball.
I'm passing to Charles.
There's only Wilson to beat.
Shoot, Charles!

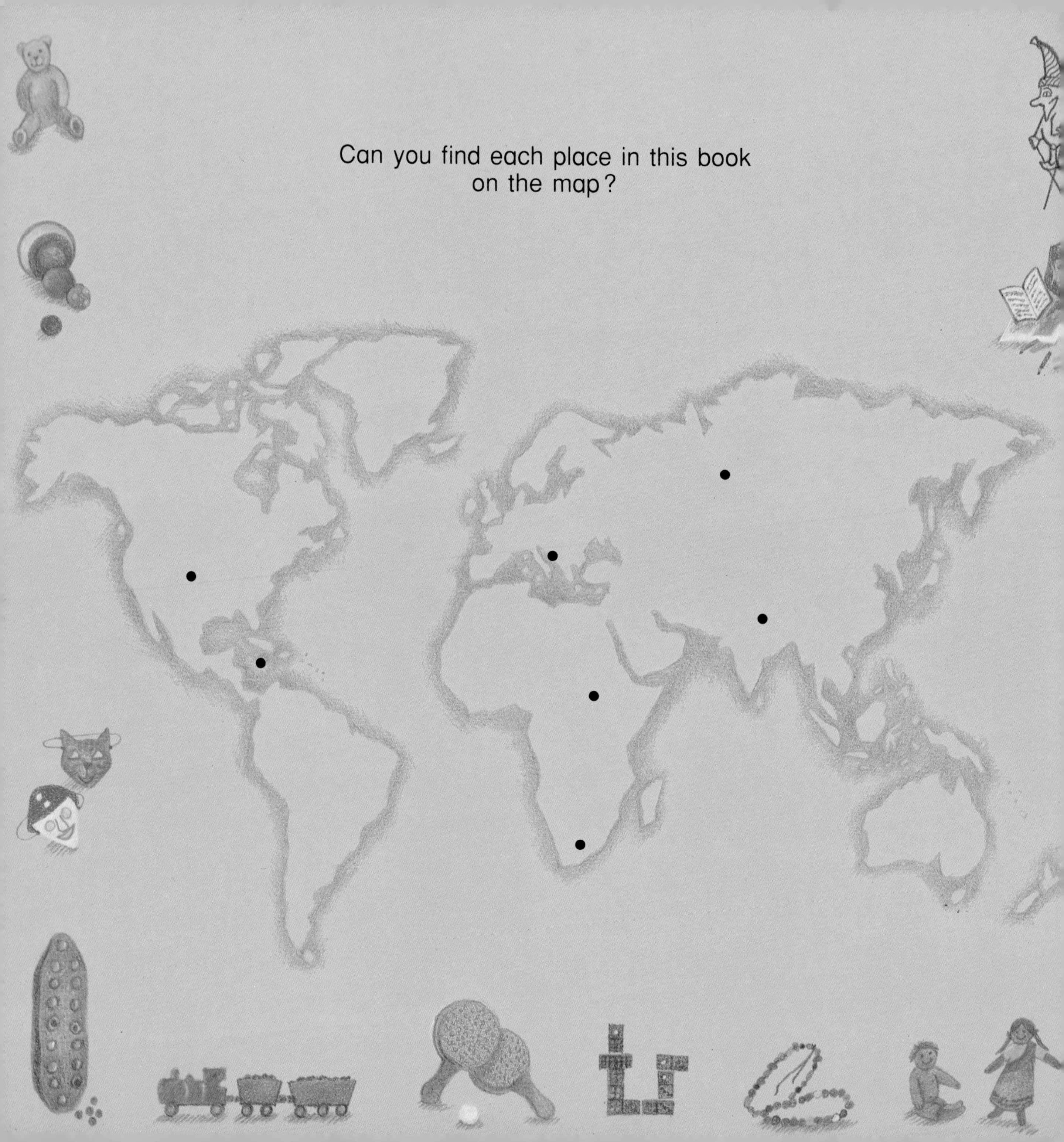

Can you find each place in this book
on the map?